I0765556

Edwin Kim

Illustrated By
Mayara Nogueira

Tae watches a popular band perform and witnesses the exciting energy of the crowd. It's now his turn on stage, and the audience becomes dead silent. To his surprise, they make fun of Tae, and he runs away in sadness. He always felt different, but never expected to feel so rejected.

While alone, he hears a voice. He follows the voice and finds Ruby, the robin. Ruby tells Tae about Tiger Town - a place where everyone looks just like him. Immediately, he decides he must travel there. Will he make it to Tiger Town? Will he feel truly accepted? Read to find out more!

Tae the Tiger was feeling very strange.
He felt tingly and twitchy.
Shivery and sweaty.
His head was swimming, and his
tummy was full of butterflies.
Tae wasn't sick, and he wasn't sad.
He was feeling nervous and really
excited at the same time.

Today was the day!
It's, "HORSE CITY'S GREATEST TALENT SHOW."
And Tae would perform for the very first time.

6

HORSE CITY'S GREATEST SHOW
7

Backstage, Tae waited for his turn.
He peaked out at the crowd.
There were hundreds of horses!
They were dancing and cheering.
The Canyon Stallions were performing
their hit country song.
The crowd went wild!
They were the most popular band in Horse City.

When their turn was over, they bowed and came backstage.
Spotting Tae, they started poking fun at him.
"Do you really think a weirdo like you should be here?"
The Canyon Stallions were always cruel to Tae the Tiger.
But, he didn't listen to them.
Tae was about to perform.

11

Tae picked up his guitar and walked onstage.
The lights were bright and the crowd was in anticipation.
Tae sat down, took a deep breath and began to play.
His claws moved with skill and grace over the strings
He was plucking and strumming a fantastic tune.

Tae played his blues song with his whole soul.
When his song was over, he looked at the crowd.
He hoped they would cheer and clap.
But, the crowd just stared at Tae
with big eyes and long faces.
Tae's tawny cheeks turned bright red!
As quickly as he could, he left the stage.

15

Backstage, the Canyon Stallions began to mock Tae.
They pointed and laughed as he ran away.

Tae didn't stop running until he reached the river.
This place always made him feel safe and peaceful.
And the sounds of the river helped Tae feel less lonely.
Tae's teardrops rippled in the water as he looked at his reflection.
"Where do I belong?" asked Tae.
"Rumble-bumble," said the River.
"You always say that," sighed Tae.
"Am I the only tiger in the world?" asked Tae.
"Of course not," said the River.

Tae was filled with such fright, he ran away from the river!
The river had never really spoken before!
"R-r-r-river?" stuttered Tae as he peaked at the river.
"Ruby!" said the voice, "And I'm not a river, I'm a robin."
Just then, a beautiful bird hopped down from
a nearby branch and beamed up at Tae.
"Oh, howdy there, little bird."
"There's a whole town of tigers!" Ruby sang.

"Really?" Tae's heart was thumping in his throat.
"Yup!" said Ruby, "Just across the desert,
through the forest, and over the ocean."
"I thought I was all alone," said Tae.
"Well, you're not alone anymore," chirped Ruby
"I'm here and I'll show you the way to Tiger Town!"

So, off they went across the desert.
Tae practiced his guitar as they traveled.
And to his surprise, Ruby sang along.
Her voice was sweet and soulful.
She harmonized beautifully with Tae's guitar.

Finally, they made it across the desert and found themselves in Elephant Empire.
"Wow! You have a mighty fine voice," said Tae.
"And I love the way you play guitar!"
"Look!" said Tae. He pointed at a poster.
"Let's perform together!"

OPEN
MIC ♫
IGHT
GLUE
27

Later that night, they arrived at the music club.
The building rumbled with the noise inside.
The music was so loud, the club nearly jumped
straight off the ground!!
It almost caused an earthquake!

Inside, Ruby and Tae were surprised by what they saw.
Elephants jumping and bumping!
Headbanging and moshing!
The band played heavy metal music, and the elephants
were even heavier!

It was Tae and Ruby's turn to perform.
So, they took the stage and played their sweet song.
The elephants stopped talking, jumping, and thumping.
They stared at the Tae and the Ruby.
And then they did the most horrible thing.
They began to boo!
They didn't like the blues music.
They couldn't headbang to it.

Tae and Ruby left the club feeling disheartened.
"Don't worry, Tae," said Ruby, "We'll find a place to belong."
This made Tae feel a little better.
"Yeah, Ruby," purred Tae.
"Let's giddy up on out of here."

32

As they walked away from Elephant Empire,
they heard a thumping coming closer and closer.
Then they saw a great big elephant running after them.
"Wait! Wait!" Tae and Ruby waited for the elephant
to catch his breath.

33

"Your music..." huffed the elephant.
"I've never felt so alive! What do you call it?"
"Why, it's called the blues, good fellow,"
said Tae with a wink.
"It soothed my soul!"
"My name is Elliot and your music
 is just what I've been looking for!"

Elliot took out a shiny saxophone.
"No one in the Elephant Empire ever liked my music either."
And then Eilliot began to play the saxophone.

The smooth music washed over them as they listened in wonder.
Tae and Ruby looked at each other with twinkling eyes.
They cheered for Elliot when he finished his song.
"That was amazing!" said Ruby.
"We would be honored if you
joined us on our journey," said Tae.
All three of them were overjoyed!

And so, off they traveled through the forest,
singing tunes all along the way.

When Tae, Ruby, and Elliot came out the other side of the forest,
they discovered Kangaroo Kingdom.
There was a lot of commotion in the kingdom.
Everywhere you looked, kangaroos were rushing around.
They were carrying things, making food, hanging up
decorations, and lighting lanterns.
Everyone was excited and busy.

Tae saw two kangaroos hanging a large sign.
Tae nudged Ruby and Elliot, and they all agreed
to perform at the carnival.

42

kangaroo Kingdom
KARAOKE CARNIVAL

That night, they took to the stage.
They had chosen a wonderful blues song
for their performance.
Their performance was perfect.
But, when they had finished their song, the
kangaroos did the most unexpected thing.
They began to laugh.

44

They thought the three friends were funny-looking.
They had never seen such a strange band.
The kangaroos laughed and laughed.
There were kangaroos holding their bellies,
kangaroos rolling around on the floor,
and kangaroos pointing at the three friends.

Elliot blushed.
Ruby wanted to cry.
Tae felt very uncomfortable,
so they left the stage.

Outside, a kangaroo hopped over to the miserable trio.
"Hi! I'm Kendall! Why are you so sad?"
"They made a fool of us!" complained Tae.
Kendall said, "I wish I had a crew, even if they were
different looking."

The three friends looked at each other.
They hadn't thought of it like that.
"Don't you have any friends?" asked Tae.
"Not a single one," sighed Kendall sadly.
"Well, the more the merrier!" chuckled Tae.
"Oh, really? Really do you mean it?"
Kendall the Kangaroo couldn't stand still.
She hopped up with joy.

Her big feet and strong tail drummed on the floor.
"Hey now, that's a pretty nifty beat
 you got going there!" cheered Tae.
The four new friends sang while leaving
the Kangaroo Kingdom.
They hopped onto a boat and
began their voyage over the ocean.

At long last, Tae arrived on the shores of Tiger Town!
He could hardly believe his eyes!
There were strong tigers and petit tigers,
grandparent tigers and tiny baby tigers,
white tigers and blazing red tigers.
Tigers here and tigers there.

52

Tae had never seen another tiger in his life
and now there were tigers everywhere!

53

"Howdy there!" said Tae to the first tiger he met.
He tipped his hat to the second
and waved at the third.
"Howdy ma'am, howdy sir!
How are y'all doing on this fine day?"
Tae was so excited, he didn't notice
the curious crowd following him.

When he reached the center of town he saw all the tigers.
"Y'all want to be my friends?"
I've come such a long way to find ya'll!"

"What is y'all?" asked one little tiger.
"Why is he wearing that goofy hat?" asked another.
The tigers of the town couldn't understand
Tae's bizarre accent and his cowboy clothes.

Tae didn't know what to say.
He saw all the faces frowning at him.
He was the strangest tiger they'd ever seen.
Tae wished he could just disappear.
But, something else happened.

Tae felt a gentle and strong arm wrap
around his waist and lift him into the air.
It was an elephant's trunk!
Elliot the Elephant put Tae
on his back with Kendall.
Ruby flew up to Tae's shoulder
and the four of them marched
straight out of Tiger Town.

They stopped on a hill far away from the crowd.
Tae was very quiet, but his friends knew his heart was hurting.
So, they sat beside him in silence and watched
the sun set over the sea.

"I thought I would find my home here," mumbled Tae.
"I'm sorry," said Ruby and nestled upon Tae's head.
Elliot put his trunk on Tae's shoulder and
Kendall patted his back.

Slowly, but surely, Tae felt
something sing in his soul.
It was warm and wonderful.
It started in the bottom of his
belly and bubbled up to the top of
his head and down to the tip of his tail.
What was this strange feeling?

"This is home," whispered Tae carefully.
His friends looked at him with wonder.
"You mean Tiger Town?" asked Kendall.
Tae shook his head.

"No, you are my home! The three of you!"
The friends looked at each other with joy.
"I came on this journey to find a place to
 belong and I did! But home isn't a place."
"It's with y'all" shouted Ruby.
"Right, you are, Ruby! Right, you are!"

Elliot wrapped his trunk around all
of them at once and squeezed
as hard as he could.
They laughed and cried and
chatted and sang!
"Where to next?" asked Ruby.
"Anywhere! As long as
it's with y'all!"cheered Tae.

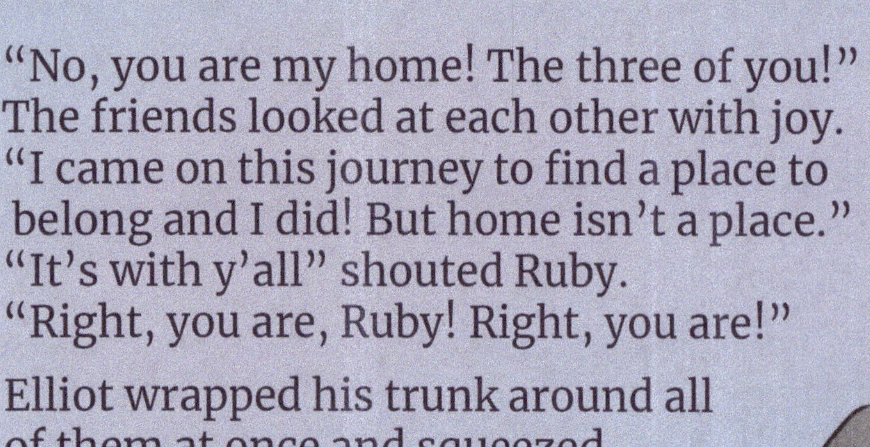

"If the four of us needed a place to belong, I bet there are four other people who also need that," said Tae.
"And another four," added Ruby.
"And four more," said Elliot.
"I bet there are hundreds of people out there who need a home," said Kendall.

65

A PLACE
TO BELONG

Some time later, on the banks of the river
where Tae first met Ruby,
stood a small but proud music club.
On the door hung a sign
"A PLACE TO BELONG"

Animals came from all around
the world to visit this marvelous place!
To enjoy the band, dance, rejoice, and just be themselves.
It didn't matter how small, how tall, how silly, fluffy,
or how different they looked.

Everyone was welcome in Tae's special place.

Author
Edwin Kim
edwinkim.co

Edwin Kim is a creative
entrepreneur who loves to
create inspirational books that
can bring valuable lessons to
the next generation. He happily
creates stories and loves
to bring his ideas to life.

Illustrator
Mayara Nogueira
artstation.com/mayaranogueira

Mayara is passionate about the
world of illustrated books.
She loves drawing animals,
historical and fantasy themes.